For the Kees family

*No dogs (picture book or otherwise) were harmed in the making
of this book, but never give human treats to real dogs!*

VIKING
An imprint of Penguin Random House LLC, New York

First published in the United States of America by Viking,
an imprint of Penguin Random House LLC, 2023

Copyright © 2023 by Jacob Grant

Penguin supports copyright. Copyright fuels creativity, encourages diverse voices,
promotes free speech, and creates a vibrant culture. Thank you for buying an authorized
edition of this book and for complying with copyright laws by not reproducing, scanning,
or distributing any part of it in any form without permission. You are supporting writers
and allowing Penguin to continue to publish books for every reader.

Viking & colophon are registered trademarks of Penguin Random House LLC.

Visit us online at penguinrandomhouse.com.

Library of Congress Cataloging-in-Publication Data is available.

Manufactured in China

ISBN 9780593117699

1 3 5 7 9 10 8 6 4 2

HH

Design by Kate Renner
Text set in Caecilia Com and Harmonia Sans Pro

The art for this book was made using charcoal, crayon, pencil, and cut paper,
then colored digitally.

NO FAIR!

Jacob Grant

VIKING

Jump on your bike, Pablo.
Today is Market Day!

Yes! Market donuts!

After shopping, we
can have a donut.

Come on, Pablo,
I'll race you there!

It's not a fair race, Dad.
This bike is too small.

You better pedal
fast, then!

Let's go, Waffles!

Waffles?

I never get to win our games.
You're too big. It's not fair.

Pablo, you might be smaller,
but you are quick!
And I don't always win.

You won both of our games yesterday.

We were just playing for fun!

You know what's really fun? Market donuts!

After shopping, Pablo.

NO FAIR!
I never get things when I want.

We may not have treats now, but we will have treats later.

That is fair.

So we just need to finish shopping, and then we can have donuts?

I can help!

Too much,
Pablo.

Too many.

Way too heavy.

NO FAIR!
I never get to choose
the good stuff.

If you can't carry it home, you can't choose it.

That is fair.

I can carry these!

Put those back, Pablo.

NO FAIR! I never get to be in charge.
Not shopping. Or cooking. Or doing anything fun.

Pablo, I'm in charge because I'm your dad.

But you can be in charge of ordering two hot ciders.

Two jumbo ciders,
please!

He will have
the kid's cup.

NO FAIR!
NO FAIR!
NO FAIR!

What if you could never choose what you want?

What if you could never win our games?

What if you were the kid and I was in charge?
Would that be fair?

I know, Pablo. Being small is not always fair.

When you're big, you'll find even more things that are not fair.

But we can always try to make it right.

Things aren't always fair for you either. Are they, Waffles?

All finished!
Now, who will help me eat
these delicious donuts?

Thanks, Dad!

Much more fair!

Come on, Dad,
I'll race you home!

NO FAIR!

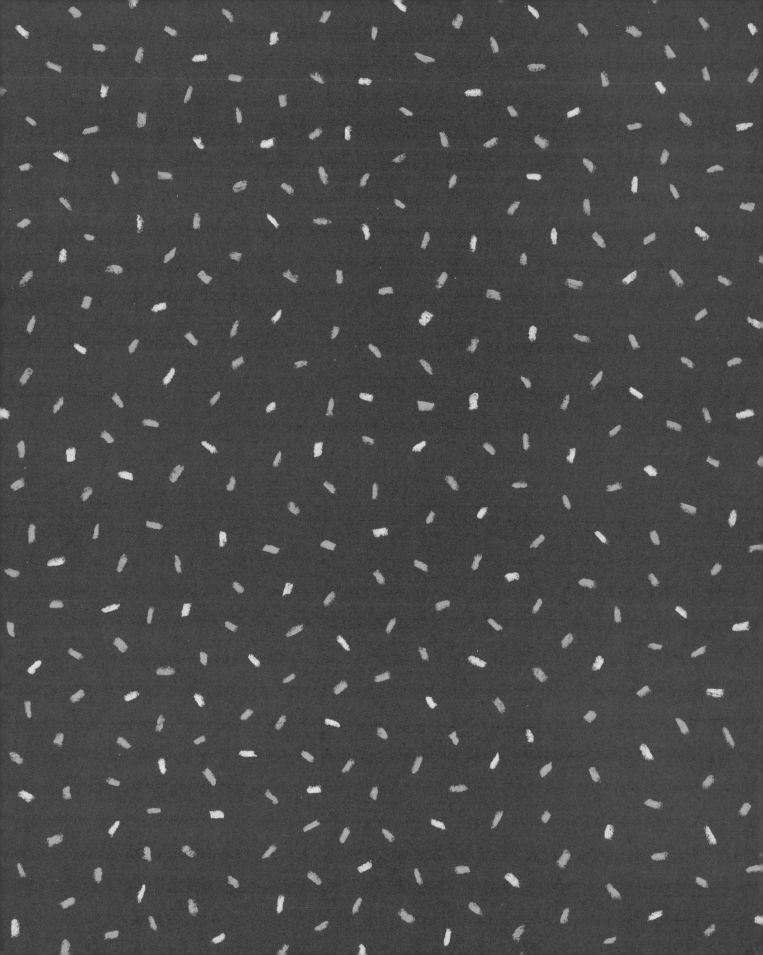